Pool PANIC

BY JAKE MADDOX

text by Leigh McDonald
illustrated by Katie Wood

STONE ARCH BOOKS
a capstone imprint

Jake Maddox Girl Sports Stories are published by Stone Arch Books
a Capstone imprint
1710 Roe Crest Drive
North Mankato, Minnesota 56003
www.mycapstone.com

Library of Congress Cataloging-in-Publication Data

Maddox, Jake, author.
Pool panic / by Jake Maddox ; text by Leigh McDonald ; illustrated
by Katie Wood.
pages cm. ~ (Jake Maddox girl sports stories)

Summary: Jenny loves swimming, and her best friend has
finally convinced her to join the school swim team — but when she is
confronted by a crowd of spectators in competition, she freezes up.

ISBN 978-1-4965-2618-2 (library binding) ~ ISBN 978-1-4965-2620-5 (pbk.)
~ ISBN 978-1-4965-2622-9 (ebook pdf)

1. Swimming~Juvenile fiction. 2. Swim teams~Juvenile fiction.
3. Performance anxiety~Juvenile fiction. 4. Self-confidence~Juvenile fiction.
5. Teamwork (Sports)~Juvenile fiction. [1. Swimming~Fiction. 2. Anxiety~
Fiction. 3. Self-confidence~Fiction. 4. Teamwork (Sports)~Fiction.]
I. McDonald, Leigh, 1979- author. II. Wood, Katie, 1981- illustrator. III. Title.

PZ7.M25643Pr 2016
813.6~dc23
[Fic]
2015024019

Designer: Kristi Carlson
Production Specialist: Lori Barbeau

Artistic Elements: Shutterstock

Printed in the United States of America in Stevens Point, Wisconsin.
092015   009222WZS16

TABLE OF CONTENTS

Chapter One

SUMMERTIME SWIMMING

"Race you to the pool!" Rachel shouted.

"No running!" Jenny called back.

Jenny smiled as her younger sister Rachel walked as fast as her little legs could go toward the community swimming pool. Sun sparkled on the clear water. It was August, and in just a few days summer would end, and Jenny would be starting sixth grade.

"Hey, Jenny!" a girl shouted.

Jenny looked over to see her friend Maya waving from the deep end. Jenny smiled and waved back at her, then turned to find Rachel. Her little sister was already starting down the steps into the pool.

"Wait up, Rachel!" Jenny shouted. She motioned for Maya to join them in the shallow end. Jenny walked down the steps and let herself slide under the cool water. "Ahhhh," she said as she popped back up. "I love swimming!"

"Me too," Maya said, swimming up to her. "In fact, I think I'm going to join the swim team this year."

"Oh, really?" Jenny asked as she waded through the water toward Rachel.

"Yeah," Maya said. "It'll be fun. I mean, we've spent all summer in the pool, why not keep it up?"

Jenny frowned. "I don't know," she said. "I love swimming, but I don't like competition. It always makes me nervous."

"But you'd be great," Maya insisted.

"Yeah, you're super fast!" Rachel agreed as she dog-paddled past the two friends.

"Maybe," Jenny said, twisting a strand of wet hair around her finger. "I'll think about it."

"Just don't take too long," Maya cautioned. "School starts next week, and tryouts won't be long after!"

* * *

The girls stayed at the pool all afternoon, swimming until the sun was high in the sky. Rachel sat on the edge of the pool while she ate a snack and kicked her legs in the water. Maya and Jenny floated in the water nearby, talking about what middle school would be like.

Suddenly, Maya stood up in the water and poked Jenny in the ribs. "Race ya!" she shouted, taking off toward the opposite end of the pool.

Jenny laughed and quickly flipped over. She cut through the water with powerful strokes. Soon she caught up to Maya and then easily passed her. Jenny grabbed the wall a couple of seconds before her friend.

Maya came up from the water, grinning. "Ha! See? You have to join the team with me," she said. "You're a great swimmer. It would be so much fun!"

Jenny rolled her eyes but smiled. "Okay, fine," she said. "I guess as long as we do it together, it'll be fun."

"Yay!" Maya shouted, giving her a big, wet hug. "Swim team, here we come!"

Chapter Two

TIME FOR TRYOUTS

On Tuesday afternoon, Jenny stood with Maya and several other girls by the side of the school's indoor pool. They were waiting for the swim team tryouts to start. The room echoed with happy chatter, and the smell of chlorine hung in the air.

Jenny adjusted the straps of her new red swimsuit and wiggled her toes on the wet deck. She breathed in and out and tried to settle her nerves.

Maya noticed her fidgeting. She linked her arm through Jenny's. "Don't worry, you've totally got this!" she said.

"We'll see," Jenny replied. She looked around the pool. Everybody was busy talking with their friends. No one seemed to be that competitive, which helped her relax a little.

Just then, a woman in a black swimsuit and track pants came through the door. She picked up the sign-up sheet, quickly looked it over, and then blew her whistle.

"Hi, girls," she said. "I'm Coach Turner. Is everybody's name on this list?" She held up the sheet, and all the girls nodded. "Great, then let's get started. When I call your name, please enter the pool. Swim one length of the pool freestyle, and then come back swimming backstroke. First up, Anna Markham."

A girl in a green swimsuit walked over to the pool, slid into the water, and began swimming along the lane. Jenny noticed that only a few of the other girls were watching. Almost everyone else began whispering to their friends again.

In the water, Anna reached the end of the pool and flipped over onto her back. She swam slowly back toward the group.

"See?" Maya whispered in Jenny's ear. "It'll be a piece of cake."

Anna climbed out of the pool and removed her goggles. Several girls gave her high fives.

"Nice job," the coach said. "Larissa Johnson, you're up!"

Jenny watched as girl after girl took her turn in the pool. Then, after the sixth person, the coach finally called out, "Jenny Brown."

A little butterfly flipped in her stomach, but Jenny walked over to the pool and got into the water. After adjusting her swim cap and pulling down her goggles, she kicked off. Jenny felt calm as she easily moved through the water. It seemed like the other end of the pool was beneath her feet in a flash. Jenny flipped and then backstroked toward the coach with strong, even strokes.

"Very nice!" Coach Turner said when Jenny arrived back at the starting wall. The coach smiled and made a note on the sheet. Some of the other girls clapped.

Jenny pulled herself out of the water with a big grin on her face and hurried back over to Maya. "That was easy!" she exclaimed.

Maya patted her shoulder. "I told you so," she replied. "You were awesome!"

Jenny blushed. "Thanks," she said. She liked these girls and the coach. Trying out for the swim team was starting to seem like a pretty good idea after all.

* * *

Two days later, Jenny joined a cluster of kids around the bulletin board in the gym hallway. Team assignments for all of Jackson Middle School's fall sports had been posted. She found the swimming list and moved closer. Anna Markham . . . Maya Granger . . . Jenny Brown!

Jenny hopped up and down with excitement. She was on the Knights swim team!

Chapter Three

PERFECT PRACTICE

"Hey, Larissa! Hi, Anna!" Jenny called out to her teammates. They turned around and waved her over. Jenny grinned as she jogged up to the cluster of girls already waiting for practice to begin.

It was the Knights' second week of practice, and Jenny was feeling good about joining the team. All of the girls were really nice, and they'd made her feel so welcome — she hadn't felt nervous once!

As usual, they would be starting in the gym. They always did some warm-ups and stretching before getting into the water.

"Okay, ladies," Coach instructed, "let's start with squats. Stand with your feet shoulder-width apart, bend your knees as deeply as you can, and hold your arms straight out in front of you. Let's do ten."

Jenny and the other girls spread out and started their warm-up exercises. Once they'd gotten nice and loose, they went to the pool and began their swimming drills.

When her turn was up, Jenny jumped in and swam a 100-yard freestyle course. The team was working on counting their strokes and trying to take fewer, but more powerful, strokes each lap. By her last lap, Jenny was crossing the length of the pool with three fewer strokes than on the first lap.

When Jenny climbed out of the water, Larissa, a swimmer from last year's team, was waiting on the deck for her turn. "Wow, Jenny, your freestyle is really strong!" she said.

"Thanks!" Jenny replied with a smile. She went to sit on the bench as another group of girls ran the drill. Maya came over and plopped down next to her.

"You looked great out there," she said. "You were the fastest in your group, for sure. How many strokes did you cut?"

"Three," Jenny said.

Maya whistled. "Nice!" she said. "Keep swimming like that, and you'll help us win meets for sure!"

* * *

At the end of practice, Coach gathered the girls on the benches.

"Our first meet is on Friday," she told them. "Make sure you arrive early so that you have time to get settled in before warm-ups. I'll be waiting for you poolside. You're all doing a beautiful job here, and I'm sure you'll do great at the meet."

The girls cheered and ran to the locker room to change. Jenny was starting to feel excited about the swim meet. Practice was so much fun, and she loved being on the team. Maybe the competition would be fun too! She felt ready to give it a try.

Chapter Four

FREEZING UP

On Friday afternoon, Jenny walked into the swimming arena and suddenly stopped in surprise. There weren't just swimmers and coaches here. Parents, siblings, and friends filled the bleachers.

Jenny gulped nervously. *I was so not expecting a crowd!* she thought.

"Jenny!" Maya called.

Jenny looked around and spotted her friend at the end of the hallway. She sighed in relief and went to join her teammate.

Maya grabbed Jenny's hand and started pulling her toward the locker rooms. "Isn't this exciting?" she asked. "Our first meet! Are you ready?"

Jenny shook her head. "I don't know," she said. "I had no idea there would be so many people watching. I didn't even ask my parents to come because I thought they'd make me nervous!"

Maya swung through the locker room door. "I'm sure you'll be fine," she said. "You've been doing great in practice."

Jenny nodded and forced a smile, then went to a bench. She already had her swimsuit on underneath her street clothes, so she quickly pulled them off and stuffed everything into a locker. She took a deep breath, then linked arms with Maya. Together they made their way out to the pool.

The 200-yard medley relay was the first event of the meet. Four swimmers would each swim to the other side of the 25-yard pool and back. Each girl had to swim a different stroke in a specific order — backstroke, breaststroke, butterfly, and freestyle. Jenny would be swimming the last leg.

Maya was up first, swimming the backstroke. She took her place on the starting block, alongside a girl from the opposing team. The swimmers waited for the starting buzzer to sound.

BZZZZZ!

The buzzer made Jenny jump as Maya dove off the block. "Get it together, Jenny," she whispered to herself.

Larissa was ready to go next. As soon as Maya's hand touched the pool wall, she flew into the water and began swimming with a picture-perfect breaststroke.

A few seconds later, Jenny heard the splash of the other team's swimmer diving into the pool. The Knights were ahead!

Jenny's eyes drifted up to the stands. The number of people seemed to have grown when she wasn't looking. It felt like a hundred eyes were on the two swimmers. Jenny hardly noticed Sarah, one of her other teammates, jumping in for the butterfly portion of the relay.

"Jenny, get ready," Coach whispered loudly.

Jenny felt her skin crawl with nerves. Butterflies went crazy in her stomach. She stepped onto the starting block and got into position. Her hands were shaking.

Right after Sarah touched the wall, Jenny dove in and began to swim freestyle across the pool. Freestyle was her favorite stroke, and she always swam it quickly in practice, but now her arms and legs felt like lead. All she could think about were the people watching her every move. The other side of the pool felt like it was miles away.

When she was a few strokes from the finish line, Jenny suddenly heard cheering from the other team. She'd been so slow and distracted that their opponents had caught up and won!

Jenny climbed out of the pool, her face red with embarrassment. "I'm sorry, guys," she said. "I don't know what happened."

"Don't worry about it, Jenny. It's only your first meet!" Larissa reassured her. Maya and Sarah nodded and hugged Jenny.

Coach wrapped a towel over Jenny's shoulders and gave her a pat on the back. "You'll settle in," she said. "Just take a deep breath and focus on your next event, okay? You can do this."

But Jenny couldn't focus on the 200-yard freestyle relay either. Her swimming was still slow and sluggish. She couldn't think about anything except all the people watching her and how embarrassed she felt.

I'm letting my friends down, Jenny thought as she got out of the pool after another bad performance. Her teammates tried to encourage her, but Jenny's heart was sinking fast. *I never should have joined the swim team.*

Chapter Five

OUT OF THE COMFORT ZONE

The Monday after the meet, Jenny went to talk to Coach Turner before practice. She'd spent all weekend reliving her terrible performance and had come up with only one solution — she had to quit the team.

"I just can't do it," Jenny told Coach. "I wasn't sure about trying out in the first place, and after what happened at the meet . . . It was a mistake joining the team. I'll only bring everyone down."

Coach Turner put her arm around Jenny, who had started crying. "Jenny," she said, "you are an amazing swimmer. You're one of our strongest during practice. I know you feel badly about the meet, but you do belong on this team. You just had a little stage fright, that's all. We can work on that."

"Really?" Jenny sniffed. "I don't know, Coach. It was so awful."

"You just need to get used to the idea of being in the spotlight," Coach said. "Try doing something out of your comfort zone, and work on not paying attention to the people around you. Like . . . maybe you could volunteer to do the morning announcements! That'd be a good start — nobody can even see you. Then we can see how this Friday's meet goes."

Jenny thought it over. "I guess I could do that," she said, wiping her eyes. "I don't know if it will help, but I'll give it a try."

* * *

On Wednesday morning, Jenny's mom pulled up to school earlier than normal. She leaned over and gave Jenny a hug. "I'm really proud of you for giving the swim team another chance, honey," she said. "Good luck today!"

"Thanks, Mom," Jenny replied, hugging her back tightly before climbing out of the car.

Jenny waved as her mom pulled away, then walked into school. But instead of going to homeroom, she went to the front office. The principal gave her a piece of paper with the morning announcements and showed her how the intercom worked.

This isn't too bad, Jenny thought. *I can do this.*

When the time came, Jenny pushed the button. It was strange at first, thinking about everyone in the school hearing her speak. But the feeling passed quickly, and soon she was reading the school news in a strong, clear voice. After she was done, she headed to class feeling proud.

At lunch, Jenny sat down next to Maya and told her friend how the morning announcements had gone. "I hardly felt nervous at all!" she admitted.

"That's awesome," Maya said. "Now you should try something bigger. Like . . . karaoke!"

"What?" Jenny said, trying not to laugh. "No way!"

"Yes way!" Maya said. "They have it every Thursday at a pizza place near my house. We are so going. But don't worry, I'll do it with you! Ask your mom."

"Okay . . ." Jenny said. "Whatever it takes, I guess!"

* * *

Thursday evening, Jenny ate dinner with Maya's family. When they were finished, the two girls walked with Maya's mom to the nearby restaurant for karaoke.

Jenny looked around the small pizza place. A few people were there eating and drinking. In the corner, an older girl was setting up the karaoke machine. There was already a man flipping through the book of songs. When the book was free, Jenny and Maya looked through it for a song to sing together.

The man was up first, singing a loud and slightly off-key version of "Sweet Home Alabama." When he was done, the scattered crowd clapped and then went back to their pizzas.

Maya nudged Jenny with her elbow, making Jenny jump. She swallowed, took a deep breath, and went up to the girl running the machine. "'Shake It Off,' please," she said.

"Awesome," the girl replied, pulling the song up on the screen. She handed microphones to Jenny and Maya as the music started.

"I stay up too late . . ." the two friends sang together, giggling. They both were a little nervous at first, but by the end of the song they were singing loudly and even dancing around a little.

When the girls finished, the crowd clapped enthusiastically. Jenny took a little bow. Maya bounded back to the book to look for another song.

"That was great! Let's do another one!" Maya said.

Jenny smiled and nodded. "Okay," she agreed. It *had* been fun, and she'd hardly felt nervous. Maybe this plan was actually working! She would find out for sure at tomorrow's meet.

Chapter Six

READY FOR COMPETITION?

The arena buzzed with voices as Jenny made her way to the pool the next afternoon. She breathed deeply, in and out, and tried to focus on her teammates and on what the coach was saying. She tried to remember how much fun she'd had singing karaoke and what it had felt like when people applauded.

If I can sing in front of strangers, I can swim in front strangers, Jenny thought. *Right?*

Just like at the last meet, today's first event was the 200-yard medley relay. And once again, Jenny was swimming freestyle. Maya gained a small lead right away, and then Larissa widened it with her strong breaststroke. But during the butterfly portion, the other team started to gain on Sarah.

The cheers and chatter of the large crowd echoed in the arena, but Jenny kept her thoughts focused on her teammate. "Come on, Sarah! You got this!" she called from the starting block.

Sarah touched the wall just ahead of the other team's swimmer, and Jenny dove into the water and began swimming. She could feel all eyes on her as she cut through the water, but she told her muscles to keep working. She reached the opposite end of the pool and flipped quickly.

Jenny felt her cheeks beginning to burn even in the cool water. But before the worry could fully set in, she felt the wall beneath her fingers and heard the buzzer sound. The Knights had won!

Jenny looked over and saw the other team's swimmer also at the wall, looking disappointed. It had been a close race.

"Yay! Great job, Jenny!" Sarah said as Jenny climbed out of the pool.

"Yeah, way to go! See, it's only your second meet, and you're already doing better," added Larissa.

Jenny smiled at the encouragements. She wanted to feel excited, like she had after she and Maya had finished their songs. Instead she still felt nervous. They'd won, but just barely. If they'd lost again, it would've been all her fault.

The next few events were a blur. Jenny sat on the pool deck trying to cheer her friends on, but mostly she worried about her next event — the individual 200-yard freestyle. Eight laps, with all those people watching her? It would be just her and the other swimmer, no team. Jenny felt sweaty just thinking about it.

A whistle sounded, and suddenly Coach Turner was waving her over. Jenny closed her eyes for a moment. *Just focus on the swimming*, she told herself. She took a deep breath and opened her eyes, then walked over to the edge of the pool and got into position.

BZZZZZ! the buzzer sounded.

Jenny launched off the starting block, but as soon as she hit the water, her arms felt heavy. When she glanced up at the end of the fourth lap, she could see that the other swimmer had already flipped and was pulling ahead.

Jenny swam as hard as she could for the remaining laps, but her nerves were too much. All she could think about was how everyone was watching her fail. She lost the event by several seconds.

"It's okay," Coach said kindly when she saw Jenny's sad face. "We're way ahead overall. One event isn't going to make us lose the meet. Why don't you take a break on the bench?"

Jenny walked over to the bench and sat down, huddled in her towel. She looked down at her shaking hands. *Will I ever be able to compete?* she wondered.

Chapter Seven

POOLSIDE SAVE

On Sunday afternoon, the community pool was crowded with people enjoying the last few days of warm weather. Jenny had arrived early and gotten a lane so she could swim some practice laps and think about her problem.

I love swimming, and my friends, and my coach, she thought as she swam backstroke. *But if I can't figure out how to compete in front of a crowd, how can I stay on the team?*

Jenny finished her lap and climbed out of the water. The pool deck was crowded with sunbathers and kids playing. The lifeguard was down from his chair, talking to some kids who had been running too close to the pool.

As Jenny's eyes drifted across the water, she suddenly noticed something. A little girl was in the deep end, struggling to keep her head above the waves of the water. The girl bobbed up and down. There was a scared look on her face.

"Hey!" Jenny shouted to the lifeguard. But it was too loud. He didn't hear her.

There's no way I can get his attention in time, Jenny realized. Without hesitation, she dove into the water. She quickly swam over to the girl, lifted her head out of the water, and carried her to the steps at the shallow end of the pool.

"It's okay, I've got you," Jenny said calmly as she swam.

A crowd of onlookers was standing around the pool watching now. The lifeguard rushed over to meet Jenny at the steps. He took the girl from Jenny and set her down on a towel to look her over.

The little girl coughed and spluttered and then started to cry. Jenny let out a sigh of relief. The girl was upset, but it seemed like she would be okay.

"Oh, my goodness!" the girl's mother cried, running over. She hugged her daughter tightly. "I looked away for a second, and Lily was gone. What happened?"

"I think she accidentally drifted into the deep end," Jenny explained. "I saw her struggling, but the lifeguard was busy. I knew I had to act fast."

"You did a great job," the lifeguard told Jenny.

The little girl's mom reached over and gave Jenny a big hug. "Thank you so much!" she said gratefully.

"Of course!" Jenny said. She gave the mother and daughter another smile and then headed to the locker room to change.

Jenny was pulling her shirt over her head when she realized something. She hadn't thought about the crowd or feeling embarrassed even once. Her thoughts had been on helping the little girl, not on herself.

Maybe this is a clue! Jenny thought. If she could keep her focus on helping her team rather than on herself, maybe she could compete after all.

Chapter Eight

KEEPING FOCUSED

At practice on Monday, the Knights began with their usual warm-ups. As the girls stretched, Jenny told Maya all about what had happened with the little girl.

"Wow, it's a good thing you were there!" Maya said.

"Yeah," Jenny agreed, "I'm so glad I noticed her and knew what to do. It was intense, but it felt good to help. And now hopefully I can help the swim team win!"

"Yeah!" Maya shouted. "Go Knights!"

They laughed and went out of the gym to join Larissa, Sarah, and the rest of the team who'd already gathered by the side of the pool. Coach Turner was just starting to go over event assignments for their home meet.

"Jenny, you'll be swimming in three events: the 200-yard freestyle, 200-yard freestyle relay, and 100-yard backstroke," Coach told her.

Jenny nodded. Those were events she was comfortable with in practice. Now all she needed to do was stay focused for the home meet. She decided to pretend the practice was a meet. When she wasn't swimming, she spent all of her time paying attention to her teammates. She cheered them on and shouted encouragement.

When it was her turn in the water, Jenny thought about Maya and all of her friends up on the deck cheering for her. They were depending on her to swim her best! She moved through the water with quick strokes and kept her thoughts on the finish line.

Coach Turner was impressed. When Jenny touched the wall, the coach clicked the stopwatch and made a note on her clipboard. "I think you swam your fastest ever today, Jenny!" she said. "Are you going to bring all that energy to the meet?"

Jenny pulled up her goggles and looked over at her team. Maya and Larissa were both grinning and giving her a thumbs-up.

"Definitely," Jenny replied, smiling.

* * *

That night at dinner, Jenny asked her parents if they would come to the meet. She'd never wanted them to come before. She had been sure that the extra attention would make her even more nervous. But this time was going to be different. She was going to make her teammates proud, and she wanted her parents to see it.

"Of course! We would love to come," her mom said. "I'm glad you're feeling better about having an audience."

"Agreed!" said Jenny's dad. "We can't wait to see you swim."

"And win!" Jenny added with a grin.

Chapter Nine

SWIMMING FOR THE TEAM

That Saturday was a home meet for the Knights. It was also a tri-meet, meaning three teams were competing, and there were more people than usual. Almost every seat in the stands was full.

As Jenny walked out to join her team by the pool, her eyes drifted up to the crowded stands. But she quickly turned her back and started talking to Larissa about her events, not letting herself get psyched out.

Jenny watched her friends swim the first relay of the meet. She kept all her attention on the girls gliding through the water. They won the first relay by a second and a half. It was a good start.

"Event number two, the 200-yard freestyle," the announcer called through the speakers. "Swimmers, please come to the starting blocks."

Jenny took a deep breath. That was her event. She got onto the starting block and pulled her goggles down. She placed her left foot back and her right foot up to the edge of the block. Then she bent her knees and crouched down.

"Take your mark," the announcer said.

Jenny gripped the block. Her whole body tensed as she waited for the starting buzzer.

BZZZZZ!

Jenny flew into the water. Keeping her body as straight as possible, she glided through the water. She thought about the finish line and her teammates counting on her to swim her fastest. The water rushed by her.

When her hand met the edge of the pool on the final lap, Jenny heard crazy cheering from her team. She looked up and saw that the other swimmers were still several strokes behind. She'd done it!

Jenny pushed herself up out of the pool and gave Maya a wet, happy hug.

"You were on fire!" Maya exclaimed.

Jenny grinned. "We are totally winning this thing!" she said confidently.

* * *

The 200-yard freestyle relay was Jenny's next event. By the time it was her turn to hit the water, one of the other teams had taken the lead. But she didn't let that stop her. Jenny jumped in and swam with confidence, finally pulling ahead of the other swimmer on her last lap. It was enough for Anna, who was swimming the final two laps, to keep the lead and win.

The excitement was contagious. Every member of the team was giving it her all and swimming her very best. Everyone was cheering.

Jenny risked a glance up at the crowd and saw her parents grinning proudly. She gave them a little wave and then turned back to her friends. She had one more event, and she needed to stay focused.

* * *

Jenny's last event of the meet was the 100-yard backstroke. It was another solo race. After her previous two successes, though, Jenny was feeling good. It was easy to keep her thoughts on the water as she climbed onto the block.

The buzzer sounded, and Jenny pushed off the wall. Since she was on her back this time, she could see the crowd out of the corner of her eye. She turned her head slightly so that all she could see were her teammates cheering from the side of the pool.

"Go, Jenny, go!" yelled Larissa.

"You're doing great!" shouted Maya.

Sarah, Anna, and the rest of the Knights whistled and clapped.

Jenny swam even harder. She was not going to let them down.

Back and forth across the pool she went, thoughts of victory filling her mind. Jenny couldn't tell where the other swimmers were in the water, so she just focused on swimming with strong, efficient strokes and long kicks.

Before she knew it, she was touching the wall. Jenny flipped off her back and looked for the other swimmers. One girl was still finishing, but the girl in the lane to Jenny's left was also done and glancing around. It must have been close.

Both girls looked up at the board to watch for their times. Jenny gasped as the times lit up the board — she had won!

Jenny jumped out of the pool and smiled big as her friends rushed over to her. "Go Knights!" she shouted.

Her teammates cheered and crowded around her. "Go Knights!" they shouted.

Chapter Ten

THE BEST FEELING

Tuesday after school, Jenny walked up to a white house and rang the doorbell. It turned out that the girl Jenny had helped at the community pool was in her little sister Rachel's first-grade class.

The girl's mother had called Monday evening and asked if Jenny would stop by sometime. The little girl's name was Lily Baker, and she wanted to meet the person who had saved her.

Mrs. Baker opened the door. Lily was standing just behind her mom, wearing a tunic with pink hearts and matching pink leggings. She smiled shyly up at Jenny.

"Come in, Jenny!" Mrs. Baker said happily, waving Jenny inside.

Jenny followed Lily and Mrs. Baker through the house and into the kitchen. Mrs. Baker gave them both some lemonade and a chocolate chip cookie, then left the girls to talk.

"Thanks for helping me," Lily said as she munched on her cookie. "I was so scared."

Jenny smiled. "I'm so happy that I could help you!" she said. "And you know, you helped me too."

"I did?" Lily asked. Her eyes went wide.

"You did," Jenny said, nodding. "I'm on the swim team at school, but before that day at the pool, I was really scared to swim in front of a crowd. I worried about what people would think of me if I messed up, and then I got nervous and really did mess up! But when I helped you, I wasn't scared at all. It was too important to be scary. I realized that helping my team win was a little bit like helping you. When I thought about it as helping instead of performing, I wasn't scared anymore."

"Wow," Lily said. "I want to be on the swim team too! If I could swim like you, I wouldn't need anyone to save me."

"That's right," Jenny said. "You just need to practice, and you'll get the hang of it in no time. Maybe next summer, I can even give you some lessons at the pool."

"Really?" Lily said. A big grin appeared on her face. "That would be so cool!"

"Sure," Jenny said. "It would be good for the future swim team, too, right?"

"Right!" Lily agreed.

The two girls chatted while they finished their snack. Jenny went home soon after, smiling all the way. Doing her best and winning was a great feeling, but helping others was the best feeling of all!

Author Bio

Leigh McDonald lives in sunny Tucson, Arizona, with her art teacher husband, two spunky daughters, and two big, crazy dogs. Besides her family and friends, her favorite thing in the world is books — writing, designing, and especially reading them!

Illustrator Bio

Katie Wood fell in love with drawing when she was very small. Since graduating from Loughborough University School of Art and Design in 2004, she has been living her dream working as a freelance illustrator. From her studio in Leicester, England, she creates bright and lively illustrations for books and magazines all over the world.

Glossary

competition (kom-puh-TISH-uhn) — a contest where people are trying to get the same thing

contagious (kuhn-TAY-juhss) — able to spread very easily

efficient (ih-FISH-uhnt) — working well and not wasting time or energy

embarrassed (em-BA-ruhsd) — feeling uncomfortable and foolish in front of others

medley (MED-lee) — in swimming, a medley is a type of race that uses all four of the competition strokes in a specific order

reassured (ree-uh-SHURD) — helped someone feel calm and less upset

relay (ree-LAY) — in swimming, a relay is a type of race where four swimmers each swim an equal distance. There are relays in different distances and that use different strokes.

Discussion Questions

1. Competitions and big crowds made Jenny so nervous that she debated quitting the swim team. What things make you nervous? Talk about some ways to handle your nerves.

2. Jenny was worried that she was bringing her team down. Do you think that her teammates ever felt the same way? Talk about why or why not, and try to use examples from the story.

3. Swimming is a combination of team and individual events. Which do you prefer — working on a team or working by yourself? Talk about why.

Writing Prompts

1. Maya helped Jenny get out of her comfort zone by singing karaoke with her. Write a paragraph about a time you helped your friend with something.

2. We all get stressed and nervous sometimes. That's why it's important to know how to calm down and focus. Make a list of things you do when you're feeling stressed and explain why they help.

3. Although Jenny wasn't sure about joining the swim team, by the end of the story she was happy with her decision. Have you ever done something you felt nervous about at first but were later glad you did? Write two to three paragraphs about your experience.

Competition Swimming Strokes

Become a pool pro and learn more about the four competition swimming strokes!

Freestyle

Also known as the front crawl, this stroke is one of the fastest. While on your stomach, bring your arms over your head one at a time. Quickly alternate moving your legs up and down — this is called a flutter kick. The key to a good freestyle stroke is keeping your body straight and timing your breathing to match your strokes.

Backstroke

Also known as the back crawl, the backstroke is similar to the freestyle except you swim on your back. Reach back with your arms one at a time and pull them back to your thigh while flutter kicking. The backstroke is a good stroke for working out the muscles in your back.

Breaststroke

In a breaststroke, lie on your stomach and move your arms and legs in half-circles. Start with your arms straight out in front of you and then scoop them under the water and back, then push them straight again. As you push your arms straight, bend your knees and kick out — this is called a whip kick. The breaststroke is probably the oldest competition stroke, but it is also the slowest.

Butterfly

The butterfly is one of the hardest strokes to learn. While on your stomach, bring your arms over your head and out of the water, then push them all the way back to your thighs. Keep your legs together, and move them up and down in a wave-like motion — this is called a dolphin kick. The butterfly is the newest competition stroke and did not have its own separate event in the Olympics until 1952.

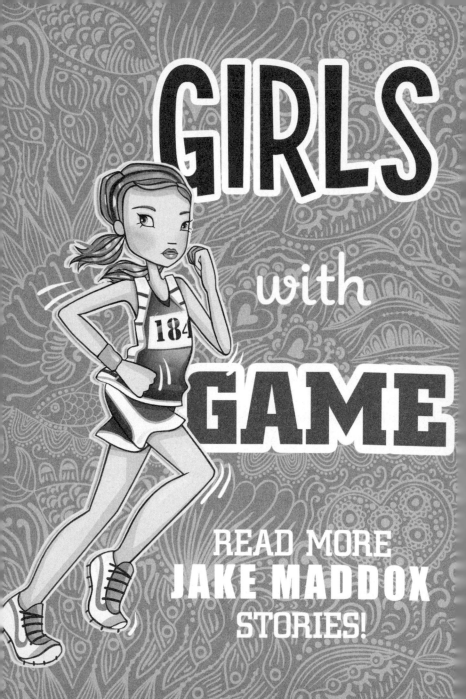

JAKE MADDOX

VOLLEYBALL
VICTORY

JAKE MADDOX

Gymnastics
JITTERS

JAKE MADDOX

SOCCER
SURPRISE

JAKE MADDOX

REBOUND
TIME

JAKE MADDOX

VOLLEYBALL
Dreams

JAKE MADDOX

HORSEBACK
Hurdles

JAKE MADDOX

SKATING
Showdown

JAKE MADDOX

DANCE TEAM
DILEMMA

JAKE MADDOX

Running
SCARED